EMMA
Every Day

Dog Watch

by C.L. Reid

illustrated by Elena Aiello

PICTURE WINDOW BOOKS
a capstone imprint

Published by Picture Window Books, an imprint of Capstone
1710 Roe Crest Drive, North Mankato, Minnesota 56003
capstonepub.com

Library of Congress Cataloging-in-Publication Data
is available on the Library of Congress website
ISBN: 9781666338768 (hardcover)
ISBN: 9781666338782 (paperback)
ISBN: 9781666338775 (ebook PDF)

Summary: Emma and her brother watch a neighbor's dog.
They soon find out how much work it is!

Image Credits: Capstone: Daniel Griffo, bottom left 28, Margeaux Lucas,
top right 29, bottom left 29, bottom right 29, Mick Reid, bottom right 28,
Randy Chewning, top left 28, top right 28, top left 29

Design elements: Shutterstock: achii, Maric C, Mika Besfamilnaya

Special thanks to Evelyn Keolian for her consulting work.

Editor's note: Throughout the book, a few words are called out and
fingerspelled using ASL. Some of these words have ASL signs too.

Designer: Nathan Gassman

Printed and bound in the USA. PO4882

TABLE OF CONTENTS

MEET EMMA

EMMA CARTER
Age: 8 Grade: 3

SIBLING
one brother, Jaden
(12 years old)

PARENTS
David and Lucy

BEST FRIEND
Izzie Jackson

PET
a goldfish named Ruby

favorite color: teal
favorite food: tacos
favorite school subject: writing
favorite sport: swimming
hobbies: reading, writing, biking, swimming

FINGERSPELLING GUIDE

MANUAL ALPHABET

Aa   Bb   Cc   Dd   Ee

Ff   Gg   Hh   Ii   Jj

MANUAL NUMBERS

0   1   2   3

Emma is Deaf. She uses American Sign Language (ASL) to communicate with her family. She also uses a cochlear implant (CI) to help her hear some sounds.

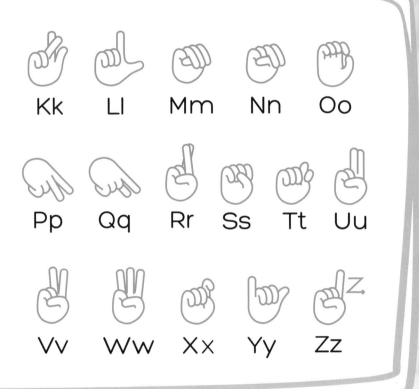

Kk Ll Mm Nn Oo

Pp Qq Rr Ss Tt Uu

Vv Ww Xx Yy Zz

4 5 6 7 8 9 10

Chapter 1

Easy Job

Saturday morning Emma woke

up early. She and Jaden had a

dog-sitting job for their neighbor,

Mrs. Stanly.

Emma was excited about watching Lily.  Plus she would earn some money!

Emma put on her Cochlear Implant (CI). Then she went to find Jaden.

"Let's go see Lily," Emma signed.

Emma and Jaden walked over to Mrs. Stanly's house. Lily was watching from the window. Lily barked and wagged her tail when they opened the door.

"She is adorable," Emma signed.

Emma put dog food in Lily's dish. Lily gobbled it up.

"Let's take her for a walk," Jaden signed.

Emma attached Lily's leash to her collar. She held tightly to the other end.

After a while, Emma and Jaden went home. Later that afternoon, they returned. Lily barked and wagged her tail.

"She is happy to see us," Emma signed.

Jaden signed, "Let's play in the backyard."

They threw a ball for Lily to fetch.  She loved running around with the ball in her mouth. Then she stopped to poop.

"Yuck!" Emma signed.

"That's part of watching a dog," Jaden signed.

He grabbed a bag and cleaned up the poop. Then they put Lily back inside, fed her, and left.

As they walked home, Jaden signed, "Dog watching is easy."

"It sure is!" Emma signed.

Chapter 2

Missing Dog

The next morning, Emma and
Jaden went back to see Lily. She
jumped up and down, wagging
her tail.

After Lily had eaten, Emma

signed, "Let's walk her again."

Emma held the leash as they

walked. But without warning, Lily

leaped forward. The leash slipped

out of Emma's hand! Lily ran off

and disappeared.

"Lily! Come back!" Emma cried.

But Lily didn't come back.

"Oh no," Emma said.

"It's okay. Let's go home and ask

Mom for help," Jaden signed.

They ran home. Their mom grabbed her car keys.

"I know we'll find her," Emma's mom signed.

But Emma wasn't so sure. Her stomach hurt. She wasn't a very good dog sitter.

Chapter 3

Hard Job

They drove around all morning.

"This is awful! We have to find her," Emma signed.

"We will," Jaden said. "Just keep looking."

They checked parks.

They asked some kids playing on

the sidewalk. They asked a mail

carrier.

But nobody had seen Lily.

After a few hours, Emma and Jaden sat on Mrs. Stanly's front steps. What would they tell Mrs. Stanly?

As Emma gazed down the street, she saw something small running toward the house.

"It's Lily!" Emma yelled.

"It sure is," Jaden signed.

"And it looks like she had fun."

"Bath time!" Jaden signed.

Emma scooped up Lily. She put

Lily in the bathtub. She scrubbed

her with dog shampoo.

Lily shook herself. She sprayed

water all over Emma.

"Yikes!  I can't get

my CI wet," Emma signed.

Jaden rubbed Lily dry with a towel. Emma mopped the floor.

"I changed my mind," Jaden signed. "Taking care of a dog *is* hard work."

"It sure is!" Emma signed.

"But we make a good team."

Jaden agreed. Lily licked Emma's

face as Emma giggled.

LEARN TO SIGN

brother

1. Place thumb on forehead.
2. Bring wrists together.

dog

Pat leg. Snap fingers.

happy

Make two small circles
at chest.

walk

Move hands up and down
like feet walking.

bathtub

1. Slide hands up chest.
2. Fingerspell T-U-B.

morning

Move hand up and
toward body.

afternoon

Move hand away
from body.

night

Move hand down and
away from body.

GLOSSARY

Cochlear Implant (also called CI)—a device that helps someone who is Deaf to hear; it is worn on the head just above the ear

deaf—being unable to hear

earn—to get

fingerspell—to make letters with your hands to spell out words; often used for names of people and places

gaze—to look hard at something

sign language—a language in which hand gestures, along with facial expressions and body movements, are used to communicate

TALK ABOUT IT

1. Would you want to be a dog sitter? Why or why not?

2. How do you think Emma felt when Lily ran away? Where there any clues in the text or art to help you know how she was feeling?

3 Jaden and Emma make a good team. Talk about someone you work well with. What traits make a good partner?

WRITE ABOUT IT

1. Write a paragraph about a job you would like to have.

2. Make a list of things you would need to do if you were watching someone's pet.

3. Pretend you are Emma and write a journal entry about watching Lily.

ABOUT THE AUTHOR

Deaf-blind since childhood, C.L. Reid received a cochlear implant (CI) as an adult to help her hear, and she uses American Sign Language (ASL) to communicate. She and her husband have three sons. Their middle son is also deaf-blind. C.L. earned a master's degree in writing for children and young adults at Hamline University in St. Paul, Minnesota. She lives in Minnesota with her husband, two of their sons, and their cats.

ABOUT THE ILLUSTRATOR

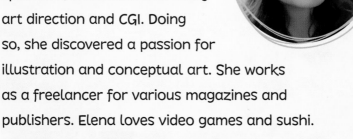

Elena Aiello is an illustrator and character designer. After graduating as a marketing specialist, she decided to study art direction and CGI. Doing so, she discovered a passion for illustration and conceptual art. She works as a freelancer for various magazines and publishers. Elena loves video games and sushi. She lives with her husband and her little pug, Gordon, in Milan, Italy.